TORO! TORO!

Also by Michael Morpurgo

Cool!
The Dancing Bear
The Butterfly Lion
Farm Boy
Dear Olly
Billy the Kid

For Younger Readers

Mr Skip
Albertine, Goose Queen
And Pigs Might Fly
Jigger's Day Off
Martians at Mudpuddle Farm
Mossop's Last Chance
Mum's the Word

Picture Books

Sam's Duck
Wombat Goes Walkabout

Audio

Kensuke's Kingdom (*read by Derek Jacobi*)
Dear Olly (*read by Paul McGann*)
Out of the Ashes (*read by Sophie Aldred*)
The Butterfly Lion (*read by Virginia McKenna*)
Billy the Kid (*read by Richard Attenborough*)
Farm Boy (*read by Derek Jacobi*)

TORO! TORO!

michael morpurgo

Illustrated by

MICHAEL FOREMAN

TED SMART

This edition produced for The Book People Ltd,
Hall Wood Avenue, Haydock, St Helens WA11 9UL

First published in Great Britain by Collins in 2001
This edition published by Collins in 2002
Collins is an imprint of HarperCollins*Publishers* Ltd
77-85 Fulham Palace Road, Hammersmith, London W6 8JB

The HarperCollins website address is
www.harpercollins.co.uk

3 5 7 9 8 6 4 2

ISBN 0 00 769325 7

Printed and bound in England by
Clays Ltd, St Ives plc

TORO! TORO!

As I was walking in the hills of Andalucia in the south of Spain last autumn, I came, quite by chance, upon a farm where they breed black bulls for the *corrida*, the bullring. The very same day I found myself on a wooded hillside looking down at the ruined village of Sauceda.

This remote village had been bombed and burned out in the early stages of the Spanish Civil War – the first time in Europe that deliberate aerial bombardment of a civilian population had ever happened. Since then, in Guernica, Warsaw, London, Dresden, Hiroshima and thousands of other cities, towns and villages all over the world, this practice has sadly become all too commonplace.

My first glimpse of that herd of magnificent black bulls, and then the sighting of Sauceda in ruins, served to inspire me to sit down and write *Toro! Toro!*. But I had some research to do first, into bullfighting, and into the Spanish Civil War. This terrible war, fought in the 1930s, was a struggle between the socialist left, the Republicans, and the fascist right, the Nationalists, for the control of Spain. After many years of vicious fighting, the Nationalists, under their fascist leader General Franco, won. Only on Franco's death, in 1975, did Spain become a democracy.

So here's *Toro! Toro!*, a story of children who lived through that war, a story of Spain, of bulls and bullfighting, of a grandfather (like me) and his grandson.

I hope you enjoy it.

MICHAEL MORPURGO
October 2001

For

Eloise,

her book.

PACO

I am the proud grandfather of a wonderful grandson – I have been for eight years. The two of us are very close. Somehow we know each other instinctively, like twins, in spite of the sixty years between us. We even share the same name. Nowadays they call me Abuelo (Grandpa), but when I was little I was always called Antonito, like him. It isn't only by his name that Antonito reminds me of me.

Until yesterday, being a grandfather had been a simple joy – all the pleasures of fatherhood, and few of the cares and woes. Then yesterday afternoon, up in his bedroom, Antonito asked me a question that had to be answered properly, honestly, and without circumvention.

It was a little enough thing that began it. It happened during the *siesta.* Antonito was bored. He was just messing around, as children do. All he did was kick a football through a window, by accident. When his mother came storming out into the garden, Antonito was standing there in his Barcelona shirt, looking as guilty as sin. He hadn't run off – he's not like that. There was no one else around except the cat and me, and we were having our afternoon nap under the mimosa tree at the bottom of the garden, well away from the scene of the crime. So, Antonio had to be the culprit. He was for it, and there was nothing I could do to help him.

"Antonito! How many times have I

told you?" I could see that chin of his was jutting already, and I knew there'd be tears welling up inside him. I could sense what he was going to say before he even said it. "I didn't do it. It wasn't me. Honest." And it was all said with such utter conviction, such determined defiance. Asked for an alternative explanation, he shrugged insolently at his mother, pursed his lips and refused to speak.

That one shrug was enough to send his mother into paroxysms of rage. He was "a careless, thoughtless, lying little toad and should be ashamed of himself". Antonito was banished to his bedroom. For some time afterwards, I could hear him crying, and then whimpering quietly in his misery and his shame. I longed to go up and console him, but had to bide my time until I was sure his mother had gone out (grandfathers have to be careful in such matters), before making my way into the house and upstairs. I knocked and opened the door.

Antonito was sitting on his bed, chin still jutting, until he saw it was me. "Hello, old fellow," I said, and went to sit down beside him. Neither of us could think what to say, so we said nothing. We often said nothing together. We were silent for some time. Then, out of the silence, came the question. "Abuelo, when you were little, did you ever do bad things? I mean, *really* bad. Did you ever tell a lie?"

"Plenty," I said. This was quite true of course, but I should have left it at that. Instead, seeking to empathise, wanting to make him feel better, I went on: "I'm telling you, Antonito, I was a whole lot better at bad things than you are. And as for lying, I was a pretty good at that, too."

He looked up at me with his wide eyes. "Honestly?" he said.

"Honestly," I replied. "Would I lie to you, Antonito?"

He smiled at that, and brushed the

tearstains from his cheeks. I felt I'd said the right thing.

"Are you going to come down now, and pick up that glass with me?" I asked him. "And then you can make your peace with your mother when she comes back, can't you?"

But I could tell he wasn't listening to me even as I was speaking.

"Abuelo," he said, "when you were little, what was the *very* worstest thing you ever did?"

I hadn't thought he would take it any further. I was on the spot now. I had a mountain of worstest things to choose from. But he'd asked me for the *very* worstest, and I knew at once what that was. I'd told no one else in near enough seventy years – not the real story, not all of it. It seemed somehow the moment to tell it; and it seemed too that if anyone had a right to know it, it was my grandson. I felt it was in some way his birthright, his inheritance. I knew too that he expected the truth from me. So I told him the truth, the whole truth.

"If I tell you something, Antonito," I said, "it'll have to be our secret. No one else must know, not until you're a father yourself, and then you can tell your own children. That's only as it should be. After all, it's our history I'm talking about – yours, and theirs too. Not a word till then, promise?"

"Promise," he said, and I knew he meant it. I could feel his eyes willing me on. So I began.

"I haven't always lived here in town, in Malaga. But you know that already, don't you? I've told you before, haven't I, how I was born on a farm, how I grew up in the countryside with animals all around me?"

Over the years I'd told him dozens of tales about my country childhood in Andalucia – he loved to hear all about the animals. But I'd promised him something much more exciting this time, and I could see he was full of expectation.

"This is not just another of my animal stories, Antonito – well, in one sense it is, I suppose. But this is the most important story I could tell you, because this story changed my life for ever. I'll begin at the beginning, shall I?"

* * * * *

I was born in a small farmhouse just outside the village of Sauceda on the first of May, 1930. There was my older sister, Maria – ten years older than me to the day – and Mother and Father. Just the four of us. We had uncles and aunts and cousins all around, of course. The whole village was like one big family. But we can skip all that. It was another birth about five years after my own that really began it all.

The farm didn't belong to Father. Hardly anyone owned the land they worked in those days – we just farmed it.

It was a hard life, but I knew little of that. For me it was a magical place to grow up. There were cork forests all around – we'd harvest the cork and cut it off the trees every nine years, to make corks for wine bottles. We had our little black pigs wandering everywhere, and dozens of goats for our milk and cheese, and chickens too. Never short of eggs for an omelette. We had mules too, for bringing the cork down from the hillsides, and horses. Everyone had horses or mules in those days. I could ride almost as soon as I could walk.

But mostly it was cows we kept. Not those lovely reddy brown Rositos you often see out in the countryside. Ours were black, black and beautiful and brave. My father bred only black bulls, bulls for the *corrida*, for the bullring. We must have had fifty or sixty of them, I suppose, counting all the calves. Magnificent they were, the best in all Andalucia, my father always said. As a small boy I'd spend hours and hours standing on the fence, just watching them, marvelling at their wild eyes, their wicked-looking horns, their shining coats. I loved it when they lifted their heads and snorted at me, when they pawed the ground, kicking up great clouds of dust and dirt. To me they were simply the noblest, the most exciting creatures on God's earth.

At that age though I had no real idea, no understanding of what they were kept for. They were just out there grazing in their corrals, part of the landscape of my life. I didn't ask such questions, not at five years old. Out in the cork forest I'd see the red deer in amongst the trees, the wild boar bolting through the undergrowth and the griffon vultures floating high up there in the sky. I didn't ask what they were there for either. Life seems simple enough when you're five years old. Then Paco came, and the war came, and the bombing planes came, and nothing was ever to be simple again.

There was a terrible thunderstorm the night Paco was born. Father asked me if I was frightened, I remember, and I said no, which wasn't true. And Maria said I was. She and I fought like cats sometimes; but I thought the world of her and she of me. So that's why I went outside into the storm with Father that night, to prove to Maria that I wasn't afraid. I followed Father's swinging lantern across the yard to the barn, hoping and praying the lightning wouldn't see the lantern and strike us dead.

The mother cow was lying down when we got to the barn, and two little white feet were already showing from under her tail. I looked on as Father crouched down behind her, took the calf by his feet, leaned back and hauled on him. There was some grunting and groaning (from both Father and the cow), but there was very little blood and it was quickly over. The calf slipped quite easily out into the world, and there he lay, shining black and steaming in the straw, shaking his head free of the clinging membrane.

"Bull," Father told me. "We've got a fine little bull." He knelt over him, lifted his head and poked a piece of straw down his nostrils. "It'll help him breathe better," he said.

The cow was trying to get to her feet. Father moved smartly away and took me with him. She was bellowing at us, and giving us the evil eye, making it very clear that she didn't want us anywhere near her calf. But try as she might the cow could not get up on to her feet. She just didn't seem to have the strength. Time and again she almost made it, but then her legs would collapse and she would be down again. In the end she gave up, and sat there breathing heavily and looking bewildered and frightened. Father did all he could to help her, but her only response now was to toss her horns at him angrily. He shouted and whooped at her, clapped her sides, twisted her tail – anything to panic her up on to her feet. Nothing would shift her.

"That calf has to drink, and soon," he told me, "or he won't live. And he won't be able to drink unless she stands up."

I joined in now, screaming at the cow to get up, slapping her, jumping up and down, but still she couldn't do it. She was stretched on her side now, completely exhausted by her efforts.

"Only one thing for it," said Father. Crouching down beside her, he stripped some milk from her udder into a bucket. Then he poured it into a bottle with a teat

on it, lifted the calf's head and dribbled the milk down his throat until at last he suckled. All the time though, he was struggling against it, fighting the bottle, fighting Father.

"We've got a brave one here," said Father. "I'll hold him, Antonito. You feed him." And he handed me the bottle.

So there I was, feeding the calf

myself. I talked to him as I fed him, and he was calmer at once. I told him how beautiful he was, how he was going to be the finest bull in all of Spain. He sucked, and as he sucked, his eyes looked into mine and mine into his, and I loved him. After a while Father had no need to hold him any more. I told Father he should be called Paco, and Father said that it was a fine and proper name for such a brave bull. But I could see Father was becoming more and more anxious about Paco's mother. She was weakening all the time. Despite his best efforts, it was only a couple of hours later that she breathed one last sigh and died. In that one night I had witnessed my first birth and my first death.

THE DANCE

Paco was soon up and on his feet. I stayed there, crouched in a corner, to witness his first staggering steps. Every few hours after that we would go to the barn to feed him. I found I had to get on to an upturned bucket, otherwise he couldn't suck properly from the bottle. I'd stand up there, wave the bottle at him and call him over to me. After only a couple of days I didn't even need to do that. As soon as I opened the door into the barn he'd come trotting over, and he'd suck so strongly that it was all I could do to hold on to the bottle. Worse still, if the teat became blocked, if he couldn't drink the milk down fast enough, he would become impatient with me and butt suddenly at the bottle as if he wanted to swallow it whole, and the bottle would end up on the barn floor.

To begin with, Father or Mother or Maria would always be there with me. Maria said it looked easy and insisted on having her turn. To my great delight Paco went wild on her and butted her up the bottom. She never asked to feed him again. They very soon realised that with me Paco was always gentle, that I could manage him well enough on my own. After that, they just left me to it, which suited me fine.

I remember those days playing mother to Paco as the happiest of my young life. Paco followed me everywhere. I'd tie a rope round his neck and take him for walks up into the cork forests. I didn't have to drag him – not that I could have anyway, for he was already far too strong for me. He just seemed to follow along naturally. He was forever nudging me to remind me he was there, or to remind me it was feeding time – again. The two of us became quite inseparable.

Then one morning, after no more than a couple of weeks, it was over. Mother tried to explain to me why it had to end.

"You've done a fine job, Antonito," she said. "Your father's very proud of you, and so am I. No one could have given Paco a better start in life, no one. But if he's to make a proper bull, a bull fit for the *corrida,* then you mustn't handle him any more. No one must. We'd be gentling him too much. He's got to grow up wild. It's what Paco was born for, you know that."

I didn't. I had no idea what she was talking about, and cared less. All I cared about was that Paco was being taken away from me.

"And besides," she went on, "he'll be better off with a cow for a mother.

Father's picked out just the right one for him. She's got a calf of her own, but she's still got lots of milk to spare – more than enough for Paco. It might take a day or two for the cow to accept him, but Father'll see to that. Paco will be fine, don't you worry."

I argued of course, but I could see it was hopeless. It was Father himself, chewing on his bread that lunchtime, who had the last say. When it came to the farm and the animals, Father always had the last say. "From now on, Antonito," he was pointing his knife at me, "you keep away from him, you understand, or else he'll be no use to anyone. Keep away. You hear me now?"

It was the end of my world.

I cried for long hours in my room, and for at least a couple of days refused any food I was offered. I made up my mind I hated Father and Mother, that I would never speak to them again and that I would run away with Paco as soon as I could. I confided only in Maria. Without her I honestly think I might have starved myself to death. She took me out to see Paco in the corral with his nurse mother. I watched him frisking about with his new-found brother and all the other calves. She assured me that Paco was happy.

"That *is* what you want, isn't it?" she said. "Look at him. Doesn't he look happy to you?" I couldn't deny it. "Well then," she went on. "If he's happy, then you should be happy, too."

So it wasn't the end of the world after all. I decided Paco and I wouldn't need to run away. I decided instead that I would see Paco from time to time, but in secret.

Not quite in secret though, for Maria was my accomplice, my stooge. We'd wait until the coast was clear, until both Mother and Father were busy in the house or on the other side of the farm. Then we'd steal out to Paco's corral. Maria would keep watch and I'd stand on the fence and call him over.

I was fearful at first that he might have forgotten me. I needn't have worried. Whatever he was doing he'd come trotting over at once and lick my hand. I think he must have liked the salty taste of it. I'd let him suck on it like a teat and he loved that. It didn't seem to matter to him that no milk came out. Sucking was enough, and when Paco sucked he sucked hard. By the time he'd finished, my hand was raw, but I didn't mind. The other calves would be milling around but I wouldn't let them have even a taste. My hand was for Paco only. Once or twice his nurse mother came wandering over and shook her horns at me, but I always kept on my side of the fence and she soon lost interest.

I'd spend all the hours I could on that fence just talking to Paco, scratching his head and having my hand sucked off. Maria was forever fearful of discovery, and kept badgering me to come away. But luckily, Father and Mother never did

find out about our secret meetings, not then, not ever.

Paco grew fast in his first year. He grew horns where there had been none, and often played at fighting with the other yearlings, mock battles which he always won. Sleek and fast, Father had already picked him out as the finest and noblest bull calf in the herd. Sometimes I would help Father move the herd to fresh pastures. We did it on horseback, with the brown and white Cabrestro bullocks in amongst them to gentle them as we drove

them. I always rode Chica, the oldest, steadiest mare on the farm. She could have done it all with her eyes closed, I expect. Even then, when the bulls were running all together, you could pick out Paco easily. He would be at the front with the big bulls, the five-year-olds, the giants. I was so proud of him, but never spoke of him to anyone but Maria. She did warn me over and over again not to become too fond of him. I remember that. "All animals have to die, Antonito," she told me. "And you'll only be sad." But I was six years old, and death meant nothing to me. I never gave it a thought. I had some shadowy understanding that it happened, but it was of no interest to me, because it happened to old people, old animals. Paco was young. I was young. So I paid my sister's words of warning very little heed.

The dawning of the terrible truth was slow at first. I was walking back home from school one day when I came across some bigger boys hanging about by the well in Sauceda. A couple of them were playing at something in the street, egged on by the others. It was a game I hadn't seen before, so I stopped to watch.

One of the boys, my cousin Vittorio, was pushing a strange-looking contraption. It had a single wheel and two handles, like a wheelbarrow. However, the wheel did not push a barrow but a crude wooden frame with horns sticking out of the front, bull's horns. It was a simulated bullfight – I could see that now. I'd seen pictures in the village café of matadors with their capes, of bulls charging them. I'd always

thought of it as some kind of dance. Vittorio was running at José with the bull machine, and José was sidestepping neatly at the last moment, so that the horns passed him by and charged only into his swirling crimson cape. And each time they all cried: *"Ole! Ole!"* It was balletic, mesmerizing, and I stayed for some while in the background, completely entranced.

Then José had a stick in his hand, and the chant went up: "Kill the bull! Kill the bull! Stick it in him! Stick it in him!"

Suddenly, in my mind, it was Paco charging the cape and the stick was a sword flashing in the sun, and there was blood in the dust and they were all cheering and laughing and clapping. I turned away and ran all the way home, the tears pouring down my cheeks. I would ask Maria. Maria would tell me it was all right, that this was not what really happened in the corrida, that it was just a game, just a dance.

I found her collecting the eggs. "It's a dancing game, isn't it?" I cried. "They don't really kill the bulls. Tell me they don't."

And I told her everything I had seen. She kissed away my tears, and did her very best to reassure me. "It's all right, Antonito," she said. "Like you say. It's a game, just a dancing game."

"And will Paco have to play it?" I asked.

"I expect so," she said. "But anyway, he won't know much about it. Animals don't think like we do, Antonito. Animals are animals, people are people."

I asked her again and again, but she became impatient with me and told me not to be silly. So I shouted at her and said *she* was the silly one, not me – a silly cow, I called her. At that she mooed at me and charged me, and I charged her back. In the scuffle we broke a lot of eggs, I remember, and Mother was furious with us both. But I went to bed reassured and unworried. We always believe what we want to believe.

Then we had news that Uncle Juan was coming to stay. Juan was the most famous person in our whole family. I'd only seen him once before at a christening, and remembered how tall and strong he stood, how wherever he was people seemed to be crowding around him. They called him *El Bailarin* (The Dancer). He was a matador, a real bulldancer. He lived in Malaga, miles and miles away over the hills. I'd never been there, but I knew it was a big and important town, and that my Uncle Juan had danced with the best bulls in Spain in the bullring there, and in Ronda too.

There was great excitement at his visit. Everyone would be coming and we'd be having a great feast. I told Paco all about Uncle Juan the evening before he came. Paco stood and listened, whisking his tail at the flies. "Maybe one day he'll dance with you in the bullring, Paco?" I said. "Would you like that?" I scratched him where he liked it, patted his neck and left him.

Uncle Juan came late the next day. We put up the long table outside, and when we sat down to eat our *paella* that evening there must have been twenty of the family there. I couldn't take my eyes off Uncle Juan. He was even taller than I

remembered, and serious too. He never once smiled at me all through dinner, even when I caught his eye. He had eyes that seemed to look right through me. The talk was all of the *corrida* in Algar the next day, of how crowded it would be, how you had to be there early to find a place.

I was just about to ask Father if I could go too when he put his hand on my shoulder. "And Antonito will be coming too," he announced proudly. "It will be his first *corrida*. He is old enough now. He may be little, but he's a little man, my little man."

And everyone clapped and I felt very proud that he was proud of me. It was all laughter around the table that evening, and I loved it.

Darkness came down about us. The wind sighed through the high pine trees and the sweet song of the cicadas filled the air. They spoke earnestly now, their faces glowing in the light of the lantens. And the talk was of war, a war I had not even heard of until that night.

Everyone spoke in hushed voices, leaning forward, as if out in the night there might be enemy ears listening, enemy eyes watching. All I understood was that some hated General from the north, called Franco, was sending soldiers from the Spanish Foreign Legion into Andalucia to attack us, and that our soldiers, Republicans they called them, were gathering in the hills to fight them.

The argument was simple enough even for a six-year-old to understand. To fight or not to fight. To resist or not to resist. Father was adamant that if we went about our lives as usual, they'd be bound to leave us alone. Others disagreed vehemently, in raised whispers, talking heatedly across one another.

Through it all, Uncle Juan sat still, smoking. When he finally spoke everyone fell silent at once. "It is all about freedom," he said quietly. "A man without freedom is a man without honour, without dignity, without nobility. If they come, I will fight for the right of the poor people of Andalucia to have enough food in their bellies, and I will fight for our right to think as we wish and say what we wish."

Soon after, I became bored with all the talk, and I was getting cold. So I crept back into the house and upstairs. As I was passing the room we had prepared for Uncle Juan, I noticed that the door was open. A moth was flitting around the lamp, its shadows dancing on the ceiling. All Uncle Juan's clothes were spread out on the bed – his matador's costume, a wonderful suit of lights, glittering with thousands of embroidered beads, and beside it his shining black hat and his crimson cape. I crept in and closed the door behind me. I could hear the drone of their talk downstairs. I was safe. The costume was very heavy, but I managed to shrug it on. It swamped me of course,

as did the huge hat which rested on the bridge of my nose so that I had to lift my chin to see myself in the mirror. Now the *muleta,* the crimson cape. I whirled it, I swirled it, I floated it and I flapped it, and all the while I danced in front of the mirror, using the mirror as my bull. *"Ole!"* I mouthed to the mirror. *"Ole!"*

Someone began clapping behind me. Uncle Juan filled the doorway, and he was smiling broadly. "You dance well, Antonito," he said, crouching down in front of me. "No bull would catch you, not in a million years. Bravo!"

"I have a bull of my own," I told him. "He's called Paco, and he's the noblest bull in all Spain."

Uncle Juan nodded. "Your father has told me of him," he said. "One day I may dance with him in the ring in Ronda. Would you like that? Would you come to see me?" He took the black hat off me, and the beautiful costume and the cape. I caught sight of myself in the mirror. I was ordinary again, not a matador any more, just Antonito.

He ruffled my hair. "You want to help me practise?" he said.

I didn't understand quite what he meant, not at first. Then he shook out the crimson cape and stood up straight and tall and near the ceiling, stamped his feet and flapped the cape. *"Toro!"* he shouted. *"Toro!"* And I charged. Again and again I charged, and each time I was swathed in his great cape and had to fight my way out of it.

At last he cast aside the cape, picked me up by the waist and held me high so we were face to face. "We dance well, little bull," he said, and kissed me on both cheeks. "Now we must both be off to bed. I've some serious dancing to do tomorrow. Wish me luck. Pray for me." And I did both.

I didn't sleep much that night. By the time I woke up, Uncle Juan had already

gone. We set off early ourselves and rode in the cart to Algar. The road was full of horses and mules and carts all going to Algar for the *corrida*. Getting there seemed to take for ever. I sat with Maria beside me, who was strangely silent; she'd hardly said a word to me all morning.

The bullring was a cauldron of noise

and heat, the whole place pulsating with excitement. As the trumpets sounded, Uncle Juan strode out into the ring, magnificent in his embroidered costume. There were other men behind him, *banderilleros* and *picadors*, Maria told me. But when I asked what they were for she didn't seem to want to tell me. Instead, she took my hand, held on to it tight and would not let go. I was suddenly anxious. I looked up at her for reassurance, but she would not look back at me.

All around the ring the crowd was on its feet and applauding wildly. Uncle Juan stopped right in front of us and lifted his hat to us. I felt so proud at that moment, so happy. Another trumpet, and there was the bull trotting purposefully out into the centre of the ring, a glistening giant of a creature, black and beautiful in the sun. Then he saw Uncle Juan and the dance began.

TORO! TORO!

To begin with the dance was like the photo in the village café, much as I had expected, except that Uncle Juan did not do the dancing. He watched from the sidelines. One of the other men did the dancing, and his cape wasn't crimson like Uncle Juan's, but yellow and magenta. The bull charged him and charged him tossing his horns into the cape. And at each pass the crowd shouted *"Ole! Ole!"* just like in the game I had seen my cousins Vittorio and José playing back in Sauceda.

All this time Maria had my hand held tight. The bull was enjoying the game, I thought, pawing the ground before he charged, snorting, shaking his head. He looked so like Paco, bigger of course, but he held his head high and proud in just the same way. Still he kept charging and the man kept dancing. It was a good game. I was enjoying it too, and shouting along with everyone else.

Then came the third trumpet. I felt Maria squeezing my hand tighter. What followed in the next few minutes I remember as a nightmare of horrors.

The mounted picadors ride in, their horses padded up, and the bull charges. The first pike goes in, deep into the bull's shoulder, and he charges again, and again. And there's blood down his side, a lot of blood, and the crowd is baying for more. He feels the pain – I can see it in his face, but he knows no fear. He's a brave and noble bull. I see what I see through the mist of my tears – the *banderilleros* teasing him, maddening him, decorating his shoulders with their coloured darts, leaving him standing there still defiant, his tongue hanging in his exhaustion, in his agony.

Another trumpet, and there is silence now as Uncle Juan steps forward and takes off his hat. I cannot hear what he says, nor do I care. I know now what is to happen, and I hate him for what he will do. He stands before the bull, erect, with his crimson cape outstretched. "*Toro!*" he cries. "*Toro!*" And the bull charges him once, twice, three times, and each time Uncle Juan draws his horns harmlessly into the cape. It seems now that the bull no longer has the strength to do anything but stand and pant and wait. I see the silver sword held high in Uncle Juan's hand, produced as if by magic from under his crimson cape. I see it flash in the sun. But then I see no more because my head is buried in Maria's shoulder.

"Take me out!" I begged her. "Take me out!" As we struggled our way through the crowd I caught a last glimpse of the bull as his carcass was dragged away, limp and bleeding, by the mules. And Uncle Juan was strutting about the ring accepting the applause, catching the flowers.

Outside I was sick. Again and again I was sick, and Maria held my head. She took me down to the tap in the village square and bathed my face. She had no words to comfort me – there were none, and she knew it. She just let me cry myself out against her.

When I'd finished, I asked her the question to which I already knew the answer. "It's what will happen to Paco, isn't it?"

"Yes," she replied, and hugged me to

her. "Don't cry, Antonito," she went on. "Paco doesn't know it. Think of it like this: it'll be just a few minutes at the end of his life, and it's all so quickly over."

I pushed her away from me. "Never!" I cried. "I won't let it happen to him, Maria, I won't." And in that moment I made up my mind that somehow, some way, I would save Paco from the bullring. "I'm going to run away with him," I said, "and I'll never come back."

I committed myself to it that same evening by promising Paco face to face. He came trotting over as usual as soon as he saw me coming. I stood on the fence, smoothed his neck and spoke softly to him. I didn't tell him what I'd seen that day – I didn't ever want him to know. "It'll be soon," I told him. "I'll take you away so you can live wild up in the hills, where you'll be safe for ever and ever. I'll work something out, I promise you." But it was to be a long time before I was able to fulfil my promise.

There were other distractions. The war was no longer just talk around a dinner table. It was only weeks after the bullfight in Algar that the first soldiers came to the village, our soldiers, Republican soldiers. Some were wounded – I'd seen them on crutches, or with their heads bandaged sitting in the café. There was talk that others were hiding in the houses in the village or up in the woods. The war was not going well for them, for us, Mother explained. We had to feed the soldiers, she said. It was the least we could do. It would give them the strength to fight again. I still had no idea what it was they were fighting for.

Almost daily now Mother would send Maria and me up into the village with eggs and bread, ham and cheese for the soldiers. We delivered it to the café, and sometimes they'd be singing and smoking and drinking. I knew they were our soldiers, but they looked rough all the same and I was frightened of their eyes, even when they smiled at me. But they let me hold their rifles and pretend to shoot, and I liked that.

At home Father wasn't speaking. We all knew what it was that was troubling him. He was against taking sides in this war. Fighting an invader – he could understand that. But Spaniard against Spaniard, cousin against cousin? It was wrong, he said, plain wrong. Besides, it would only get us into trouble with one side or the other. He wanted us to stay out of it.

But in this Mother was adamant. She would send food to the soldiers in the village no matter what he said. They were defending us, defending freedom, and she would help them. She argued cleverly, talking him round, so that although he never agreed with her, he let her do what she wanted all the same. But he was grudging about it, and morose and silent. Thinking back, I suppose it must have seemed as if we were all against him. Maria and Mother were, it was true; but I just took the food up to the village because I wanted to hear the soldiers singing again and hold their rifles.

In all this time, Paco's escape was never out of my mind. I lay awake at night trying to work out how it might be done. Every time I went to church I'd pray to Jesus to tell me the way to do it. How could I separate Paco from the fifty others in his corral, and take him away up into the hills? How was I going to do it? I thought of confiding in Maria, of asking for her help, but dared not. There was just a chance that she would tell Mother – they were more like sisters, those two, always talking heart to heart. No, I would keep it to myself. Somehow I would have to work it out on my own.

The day the idea came to me, I was driving the herd with Father to the corral furthest from the house, where there was more grass. He seemed more talkative out on the farm with me than he ever was at home. It was because of his bulls, I think, his beloved black bulls. He was always at his happiest when he was amongst them. I was riding Chica, as usual, rounding them up from behind. The herd was drifting along easily – Paco going on ahead with the big bulls – when Father rode up alongside me.

"Well, Antonito," he said, "it won't be long before you can do this all on your own, will it?"

"No, Father," I replied, and I meant it too, because even as I spoke I realised at last how it could be done, how I could set

Paco free. I knew that what I was planning was terrible, the most terrible thing I could ever do to my father; but I had to save Paco, and this was the only way I could think of to do it.

That same night I lay in my bed forcing myself to stay awake. I waited until the house fell silent about me, until I was as sure as I could be that everyone was asleep. The sound of Father's deep snoring was enough to convince me that it was safe to move.

I was already dressed under my blankets. I stole out of the house and across the moonlit yard towards the stable. The dogs whined at me, but I patted them and they did not bark. I led Chica out of her stable, mounting her some way down the farm track, out of sight of the house, and then rode out over the farm towards Paco's corral.

My idea was clumsy but simple. I knew that to separate Paco from the others, to release him on his own would be almost impossible, and that even if I succeeded, sooner or later he would be bound to come running back to the others. He was after all a herd animal. I would have to release them all, all of them together, and drive them as far as I could up into the cork forests where they could lose themselves and never be found. Even if they caught a few of them, Paco might be lucky. At least this way he stood some chance of freedom, some chance of avoiding the horrors of the *corrida*.

The cattle shifted in the corral as I came closer. They were nervous, unsettled by this strange night-time visitor. I dismounted at the gate and opened it. For some while they stood looking at me, snorting, shaking their horns. I called out quietly into the night. "Paco! Paco! It's me. It's Antonito!"

I knew he would come, and he did, walking slowly towards me, his ears twitching and listening all the time as I sweetened him closer. Then, as he reached the open gate, the others began to follow. It all happened so fast after that. To begin with, they came at a gentle walk through the gate. Then they were trotting, then jostling, then galloping, charging past me. Paco, I felt sure, was gone with them, swept along in the stampede.

I don't know what it was that knocked me senseless, only that when I woke, I was not alone. Paco was standing

over me, looking down at me, and Chica was grazing nearby. Whether Paco had saved me from being trampled to death, I do not know. What I did know was that my plan had worked perfectly, better than I could ever have hoped for.

I got to my feet slowly, amazed that nothing was broken. I was not badly hurt at all, just a little bruised, and my cheek was cut. I could feel the blood sticky

under my hand when I touched it. I had no rope, but I knew I would not need one, that Paco would follow along behind Chica and me as if he'd been trained to it.

I had in mind to go as far as I could, as fast as I could, before dawn. Beyond that I had no thought as to where we would go, nor what I would do with him. As we climbed the rutty tracks up into the hills, I felt inside me a sudden surge of elation. Paco was free and now I would keep him free. I had no conscience any more about what I had done, no thought now of what it would mean to Father to lose his precious herd of cattle. Paco would not suffer that terrible death in the ring – that was all that mattered to me. I had done it, and I was ecstatic.

Chica seemed to know the path, and she was as surefooted as a mule. I never once came near to falling off, despite my exhaustion. Behind us, Paco was finding it more difficult, but he was managing.

I felt the damp of the morning mist around us before I ever saw the dawn. We climbed on, higher and higher into the mist, until the last of the night was gone and a hazy white sun rose over the hills.

We came suddenly into a clearing. On the far side was a stone hut, most of it in ruins, and beside it a circular stone corral. I hadn't seen this one before, but I had seen others. There were several like it scattered through the cork forests, built for gathering cattle or sheep or goats. Paco followed us in and I shut the gate behind him. Both Paco and Chica at once began nuzzling the grass. I lay down in the shelter of the wall, and was asleep before I knew it.

The warming sun woke me, that or the cry of the vultures. They were circling above us in the blue. The mist had all gone. Paco lay beside me, chewing the cud and licking his nose. Chica stood, resting her fourth leg, only half awake. I lay there for a while, trying to gather my thoughts.

That was when I heard the sound of distant droning, like a million bees. There

were no bees to be seen, and nothing else either. I thought I must be imagining things, but then Paco was on his feet and snorting. The vultures were suddenly gone. The droning was coming closer, ever closer, until it became a throbbing angry roar that filled the air about us. Then I saw them, flying low over the ridge towards us, dozens of them – airplanes with black crosses on their wings. They came right over us, their engines thunderous, throbbing so loudly that it hurt my ears.

In my terror I curled up against the wall and covered my ears. Paco was going wild and Chica, too, was circling the corral, looking for a way out. I waited until the planes were gone, then climbed up on to the wall of the corral. They were diving now, their engines screaming, diving on Sauceda, diving on my home.

I saw the smoke of the first bombs before I heard the distant crunch of the explosions. It was as if some vengeful God was pounding the village with his fist, each punch sending up a plume of fire, until the whole village was covered in a pall of smoke.

I stood there on the corral wall, trying not to believe what my eyes were telling me. They were telling me that my whole world was being destroyed, that Father and Mother and Maria were down there somewhere in all that smoke and fire. I don't think I really believed it until the planes had gone, until I heard the sound of silence again, and then the sound of my own crying.

SAUCEDA

Paco was still frantic, still circling the corral in his terror, so he paid me little attention as I caught Chica, led her out of the gate and closed it behind me. Only then did he seem to realise what was happening and came running over to us.

"I'll be back, Paco," I told him. "I'll be back, I promise."

I mounted up and rode away. The last I saw of him he was looking over the gate after us, tossing his head, pawing at the ground, and then we were gone down into the woods out of his sight. For some time I heard him calling for us, his plaintive bellowing echoing around the hills. Below us the smoke drifted along the valley, as if a sudden new mist had come down.

Chica seemed to understand the urgency, for she retraced her steps at speed the whole way down, stumbling often. Where the path was at its narrowest and most treacherous, I dismounted and ran on ahead, leading her. But running or riding, my head was filled with a gnawing dread of what I might find. I longed to be there, to see Maria and Father and Mother again, and yet I was reluctant to arrive in case my worst fears proved true. From time to time I was seized by fits of uncontrollable sobbing, but by the time we reached the outskirts of the farm I felt strangely calm, as if I had no more tears left to cry.

Perhaps because I had had so long to think about it, the sight of my home in ruins, in flames, came as no shock to me. The pigs snuffled about the yard as they always did, the goats grazed busily, scarcely stopping to look up at me as I passed. I stood in the yard and watched my house burn, the flames licking out of the windows. There was a terrible anger in those flames. I could hear it in all their roaring and crackling and spitting. I did not call for Father or Mother or Maria for I knew they must all be dead. No one could have survived in that inferno. How long I stood there I do not know, but I did not cry again until I saw the dogs. I found them lying dead near the water trough. I sat down beside them and wept till I thought my heart would burst.

In time, the flames had nothing more to burn and died down. Only the walls remained, charred and smouldering. I

turned away, and with Chica following me, made my way along the road into Sauceda.

The village was unrecognisable. Hardly a house had survived. But I heard people, voices I knew. Then I saw them, faces I knew. My cousin Vittorio stood in the street with blood on his face. He was wailing, calling for his mother. There was so much wailing. Some were wandering about in a daze, mumbling to themselves.

Others just sat staring into space, tears running down their cheeks. I recognised some of the soldiers from the café. Several of them were filling buckets at the well and running across the street to a house that was still burning.

Only then, as I watched, did it occur to me there could be a chance that Mother and Father and Maria might still be alive. I began to ask after them. Vittorio didn't seem to know me. He just stared at me and kept saying over and over, "My mama. Where is my mama?" I asked everyone I saw, but no one had seen my family, no one could help me.

Then, as my thoughts gathered themselves, I wondered if I might have given them up too quickly. I should have searched for them back at home. They could have got out alive. Others had.

I rode home as fast as Chica would carry me, scouring the fields around me as I went. As I came into the farmyard I called out, but only the goats answered me. I looked in every barn, in every shed. I rode out over the fields, calling for them, calling for them, till my throat was raw, and I knew it was hopeless to go on.

I was sitting on the steps to the barn, my head in my hands, when I heard voices. I stood up. Soldiers. Hundreds of them were moving up the valley towards the farm, towards the village – not our soldiers, but other soldiers in different uniforms. If I ran for it, I would be seen before I reached the trees. The barn was my only chance.

I darted inside, and looked for somewhere to hide, anywhere. The voices were coming closer. I climbed the ladder to the hayloft, burrowed myself deep into the hay, curled myself up and was still. They were outside in the yard now, and laughing. I heard Chica whinnying and go galloping off. They were firing, whether at Chica or not I did not know. I curled myself up tighter and gritted my teeth to stop myself crying out loud.

I heard heavy footsteps in the barn below me, and a soldier's voice: "Let's burn the place down."

“Later,” came the reply, “we've more important work in Sauceda. Let's go.”

I lay where I was until I was quite sure it was safe. When at last I ventured out from under the hay, I found the whole farm deserted, except for Chica who was grazing contentedly with the pigs. I was down the ladder in a trice, and haring out across the yard. I scrambled under the fence and ran across the field towards Chica, scattering the pigs as I came. She stood still for me to mount her, and then we were away, galloping towards the hills and safety.

I rode up the same track I had taken the night before, but Chica was tired now and finding the going hard. She was breathing heavily, so after an hour or so I decided I must let her rest. I dismounted by a spring so that Chica could rest and have a drink at the same time. As she drank I looked down into the valley below, and saw the smoking ruins of Sauceda.

That was the moment the shooting began. I stood there and hid my face in my hands as the people of Sauceda were massacred. The sound of that shooting still echoes in my head all these years later. There was a terrible evil done that day. I didn't understand the nature of evil as a young boy, but I understood the loss. I understood that now I had no mother, no father, no sister, no family, no friends, no home. All were gone from me in one day. But I still had Paco. I had Chica, too. I wasn't entirely alone.

It was dusk before we reached the clearing and the stone corral again. I called for Paco as I rode up to the gate, but he did not come. He did not come because he was not there. I discovered a gaping hole in the stone wall. Paco had burst his way through and was gone. I was neither sad nor glad. Certainly Paco had been saved from the *corrida*. But all that had suddenly become very unimportant.

Exhausted, I lay down to sleep in the ruined shepherd's hut with Chica beside me for warmth. Like Chica, I had drunk from the stream nearby, but I ached with hunger, and with the pain of my loss. When I closed my eyes I saw Mother's face, and Father's and Maria's, and our home burning. I heard the shooting and the crackling of flames. I slept only fitfully, fearful of my nightmares, so that I was relieved to wake and find it was morning. But hunger was still gnawing at my stomach.

Looking back, I think perhaps it was the hunger that saved me in my early days in the hills, for it drove all other thoughts from my mind. I *had* to find food. I knew where to look – I had been out often enough with Mother or Maria picking the wild asparagus or mushrooms (I knew the good from the bad, or I thought I did), and thistles too, the thistles with the juicy stems. So, as we travelled that day, always higher into the hills, away from Sauceda, I gathered all I could find and ate it as we went. But try as I did, I could never find enough. I ate everything raw – I had no way of making fire, no means of cooking. I chewed on acorns, I plucked the fruit of the strawberry tree. I hated both, but they were better than nothing. I drank water whenever I could. When you're hungry, even water seems to fill you up, for a while at least. Worst of all, I saw food all about me in the woods – wild boar, red deer, fish in the streams. They came to tease me, I think. I tried tickling trout, but failed to catch any.

Chica of course had no problems finding all she needed to eat. She simply grazed as she went. It was she I talked to now, my only surviving companion. We slept on the forest floor, under the canopy

of the trees, in limestone caves, wherever we could find shelter. I kept always to where the forest was thick, and as far as possible from all human habitation.

I do not know, because I really can't remember, how many days or weeks we wandered the hills together. But I do know that in the end, an infrequent diet of mushrooms and thistles and asparagus was not enough. It was all I could do now to find the strength to climb up on to

Chica, all I could do to cling on. My head was swimming, and I felt overcome by weakness and drowsiness. Time and again I slid out of the saddle, and then one day I fell off and just could not get up again. I lay there looking up at Chica, at the waving of the branches, at the shifting of the clouds. I heard the wind sighing through the forest and remembered, long long ago it seemed, a lantern-lit dinner outside the farmhouse, the time when Uncle Juan came, the day before the bullfight. I remembered his words: "A man without freedom is a man without honour, without dignity, without nobility." I could hear his voice speaking to me. I could see his face. And he was smiling as he had done in the bullring, lifting me up as he'd done when I'd danced the bull dance with him at home.

Now I could feel him carrying me. He was talking to me: "You'll be all right, Antonito. You'll be all right. I'll look after you now." I thought I must be dreaming, or that we were both dead and up in heaven. I reached out and touched his face. He was real. It *was* Uncle Juan.

THE BLACK
PHANTOM

They told me later just how difficult it was to save me, to bring me back from the dead. It wasn't only that I was emaciated and wracked with fever when Uncle Juan brought me in. Uncle Juan and the others did what they could for me – but for weeks, they said, it seemed I had no wish to live. I don't remember being like that. There's not much I can remember, as I drifted in and out of sleep, but I do remember Uncle Juan being beside me. He would bathe my face with cold water. He would stroke my hair, talk to me, and try to feed me food I didn't want to eat.

I was lying in a cave, I knew that

much. I could smell the smoke of cooking, and hear the sound of people talking, moving about me, men and women and crying children. They would often come and peer down at me, close to my face. One day I heard one of them whisper to another: "It's Juan's little nephew, from Sauceda. Poor little mite. He's dying you know."

And I thought inside myself: "No, I'm not. I'm *not* dying. I won't let myself die. I want to see Paco again. I want to find him." So I started to eat for Paco, and very slowly began at last to regain my strength. And, as I did so, I began to take stock of what was going on around me.

I soon discovered that Uncle Juan was universally regarded as our leader. I could see that everyone looked to him for constant reassurance, and relied heavily on his strength of purpose and his unwavering optimism. Whenever he spoke, he inspired us and gave us hope. And hope was all we had. There might have been fifty people living up in the cave. Perhaps half were freedom fighters, like Uncle Juan. The rest were refugees hiding out in the hills, terrified to return home for fear of the soldiers, or the police, the *Guardia Civil*. Food was scarce; we had only what was brought up to us at night from the villages, or gleaned from the forest around.

I didn't have to tell Uncle Juan about the bombing of Sauceda. He knew about it, everyone knew about it, but there was no one else in the cave from Sauceda, and no word of any other survivors. I was the only one, and only I knew why that was. If I had not chosen that night to set Paco free, then I too would have been dead in the ruins of the farmhouse, or shot down trying to escape.

The more I thought of it, and I thought of it almost constantly, the less I felt I had the right to be alive. I hadn't survived just by good luck, but because I hadn't been there. I'd been away committing a dreadful crime. I'd been releasing all Father's beloved bulls into the wild, his whole pride and joy, robbing him of his lifetime's work. When I cried now it wasn't from hunger or grief, but from shame, from a deep sense of my own unworthiness.

Uncle Juan would hold me tight to comfort me. "I know, Antonito," he said one morning, wiping my tears away with his thumbs. "They were terrible things you saw. I know the pain you must feel.

Everyone here in this cave knows the pain you feel now. So cry, cry all you want. But when you've done crying, then be brave again, be my little brave bull, and come out fighting. Evil, Antonito, must be fought, not cried over. You understand me?" He smiled at me and laughed. "We are few, but we are strong. Even the beasts are on our side, do you know that? Have you heard about the Black Phantom of Maracha?"

Uncle Juan often told me stories to cheer me up, to take me out of myself. He told them well, too, and I loved to listen.

"This is not just one of my little tales, Antonito, this is true. There are patrols out in the hills – soldiers, *Guardia Civil*, looking for us. Don't you worry, Antonio. They won't catch us. We ambush them, we fight them. We send them running

like the rabbits they are. But yesterday they sent out a patrol from Maracha – maybe twenty men from the *Guardia Civil*. They thought they saw something move in amongst the trees. They started shooting. Suddenly, out of the trees he comes, the Black Phantom! You know what he is, the Black Phantom?" I had no idea. "A *nobile*, a young fighting bull. He came charging at them. And what did they do? They dropped their rifles and ran.

"But one of them didn't run fast enough, and got himself tossed in the air like a pancake. Then the bull chased the others off, scattering them into the forest. When they turned to look, he had vanished, like a phantom, a Black Phantom. They went searching for him, but it was as if he had never been there. Yet he *had* been there. There were hoof prints, the hoof prints of a young bull. What do you think of that, Antonito?"

I could think of nothing to say. I had so much to say, so much I was longing to tell him, but I could say nothing without confessing all I'd done, without betraying myself. I knew, even as he was telling me, that it was Paco. It *had* to be Paco. Paco was alive! He was out there, somewhere. He was looking for me. One day we would find each other again, I was sure of it now.

After a while, because I had to say something, I said: "That bull, he must be the bravest bull in the whole world."

"You're right, Antonito," said Uncle Juan. "And if he can be brave against all the odds, then so can I. So can you."

The story of the Black Phantom lifted our flagging spirits – everyone knew about him by now. That evening the whole cave was suddenly a happier place. I heard the sound of laughter again, and when the children got together to act out the drama, I got up and joined in. I was the *nobile*, the young bull. I was Paco. I pawed the ground like he did, tossed my head like he did, and charged around the cave; and they all screamed and ran away like rabbits, like the *Guardia Civil* in the forest at Maracha.

But the fun and games were short-lived. Later that evening, there was the sound of shooting echoing about the hills. Danger was suddenly close again. Silent now, we huddled together in our fear.

The next morning Uncle Juan called everyone together. We all had to move deeper into the hills, he told us. The soldiers and the *Guardia Civil* were getting nearer each day. There had been fighting in the valley, and the soldiers were searching the forest. If we stayed where we were we could be discovered. So began our long march, some of the

most terrible days of my life, days I shall never forget.

We only had two mules and Chica between all of us, and they were needed to carry what few blankets, what little food we had, as well as the younger children. The food very soon ran out, and then the rain came down, turning the tracks into streams and quagmires. We could only go as fast as the slowest amongst us, two old ladies, twin sisters, from Algar. Uncle Juan told the two old ladies they should ride instead of the children – I heard him – but they refused.

"It is the young that must live, Juan," one of them said, "not the old. We have had our lives. We have our sticks." And so they walked, and we children took turns to ride. Sometimes I rode Chica. Uncle Juan often gave me two small children to look after; one rode in front of me, the other clinging on behind. It was good to be riding her again, to feel her warmth and strength beneath me.

One morning, after yet another cold night in the open, we were readying ourselves for another day's march when I noticed that the two old sisters from Algar hadn't moved. They were lying together under a tree, hugging each other for warmth. Uncle Juan was crouching over them, trying to rouse them. I went over to him. I knew at once that they were dead. They lay so still, so absolutely still, one with her forefinger on her lips as if willing the world to hush. When Uncle Juan looked up at me, all the strength was suddenly gone from his eyes, and instead I saw only a deep sadness.

We buried them where they lay. Uncle Juan was never the same after that. I never once saw him smile again. All that great heart seemed to have gone out of him, but nonetheless, I still pinned all my faith, all my hopes on Uncle Juan. To me, to everyone, he was the one person who would bring us through somehow. He led us on, ever deeper into the hills, and from the top of every pass we saw always more hills, higher hills lost in the clouds. And still the rain came down. On we trudged, and as we went others joined us, more freedom fighters, more refugees, till our fifty was nearer two hundred.

One afternoon, as we came out of the woods into a narrow valley with a river running through, the rain stopped and the sudden sun warmed our backs and lifted our spirits. I remember we were singing as we came down into the valley. We saw ahead of us a cluster of farmhouses in a clearing, but it seemed as if the place was deserted.

From out of the houses they appeared, one by one at first, then in twos and threes, in their dozens, fearful, bedraggled and pale. But as they recognised who we were, as they realised we were friends, their faces lit up, and they came running. Uncle Juan and the freedom fighters were greeted like conquering heroes. Stranger hugged stranger. Friends found friends. Bound by common suffering, strangers became friends. We wept out of sheer joy that we were together, that we were alive.

Almost at once the talk was of the Black Phantom. Everyone knew of him, but only I knew who he was. Only I knew he was Paco. Every time I heard the name the Black Phantom, I felt so sure it was him, so certain that one day Paco and I would meet again.

I was making my way through the crowd of people, walking Chica down to the river for a drink, when I saw a girl standing in front of me, gaping at me wide-eyed. Maria! It was Maria! How long we clung to each other and cried together I do not know.

"And Mother? Father?" I asked her, but she shook her head and walked me to the river. There, on the river bank, as Chica drank her fill, she told me what had happened – how, when I couldn't be found that morning, she'd been sent out to find me, how the planes had come, and the house had been hit. She'd run back but there was nothing she could do. The house was ablaze. She couldn't get near it. She had looked for me everywhere, called for me, and the pigs and the goats and the chickens were running everywhere in a wild panic, and all the time the planes were bombing and strafing. All she could think of was getting away. So she ran and ran. She'd wandered the woods for days before meeting a charcoal burner, who had fed her and cared for her, and brought her here to hide up in the hills with all the others. They'd been here for weeks and weeks, she said, but there was very little food to go round and they were all terrified that the *Guardia Civil* might come.

"You won't have to worry about that any more," I told her, "because Uncle Juan is here with his soldiers, and they'll look after us."

"Uncle Juan is here!" she cried; and then she saw him and went running to him, throwing herself into his arms.

The three of us, Uncle Juan with an arm around each of us, sat together that night and we talked under the stars. After a while we fell silent, each of us wrapped in our own thoughts. That was the moment Maria asked me the question I'd been dreading. "You never told me, Antonito. Where were you when the planes came? I looked everywhere."

The lie I'd prepared came out easily. "I got up early and took Chico for a ride.

I wanted to see Paco. Then I heard the planes, and Chico just bolted. I couldn't stop her. I tried but she galloped off into the hills, and I clung on."

"Thank God she did. And thank God you went for a ride that morning," said Maria. "If you hadn't, then we'd both be dead, like Mother and Father."

Uncle Juan drew us closer. "I've decided," he whispered. "You take Chica, and you go tonight, now."

"Why?" I asked him.

"Because we are too many here. There's not enough food to go round. Because sooner or later we'll be discovered and will have to fight. We will fight, and fight as well as we can. But we are few and they are many. I don't want you to be here when it happens." Maria tried to interrupt. "No arguments, Maria. I have thought it all through. It's the only way.

"I want you to go to Malaga, to my mother's house – you've been there, Maria, you'll find the way. Kiss her for me, Antonito, and look after her. Be a son to her. Will you do this for me?"

"Yes," I said.

"Follow the river down into the valley. You'll join the road there. The *Guardia Civil* won't harm you. You are children. They have children of their own."

He led us to where Chica stood, white in the moonlight. He held us for a moment, kissed us both on the forehead, then picked us up one by one and sat us astride Chica.

"Go with God," he whispered, and we rode away along the riverbank and left him there. We kept turning in the saddle to see him, until the darkness took him from us and we were alone.

We did see soldiers, lots of them, but luckily they ignored us. Several times the *Guardia Civil* stopped and questioned us. Maria told them we were visiting our great aunt in Malaga, and each time they nodded us through. Wherever we stopped for the night people fed us and gave us shelter. If I learned one thing on that last journey, and while hiding in the hills with the refugees, it was that men and women have a capacity for kindness as great if not greater than their capacity for evil.

When at last, after many days' travel, we reached Malaga and Uncle Juan's house, I set about doing just what Uncle Juan had told me. I kissed his mother, and made myself a son to her. Together, Maria and I looked after her. I think she knew all along that Uncle Juan would not be coming home. She was strong and proud in her grief. We never did discover what happened to him. Like so many thousands of others in the Civil War, he just disappeared. But he's not forgotten.

Not forgotten, either, was the Black Phantom. Even in Malaga, in my new school, they had heard of him. There were stories of how he had been seen wandering the streets at night in Cortes, bellowing defiance, or spotted by a shepherd in the hills outside Jerez, even in the castle keep at Gaucin. He had surprised a column of soldiers, hundreds strong, near Cortes and put them to flight, and chased a *Guardia Civil* officer through the street of El Colminar. Even as a boy I knew the stories couldn't all be true – though I hoped they were, of

course. But the Black Phantom's survival and the tales of his triumphs kept hope alive even in the depths of our despair as the war was lost. I kept in my heart the hope that one day I might see Paco again, but as time passed it became only the faintest of hopes, based on a story I only half believed.

Great Aunt Nina was as good a mother to me as an old lady could be, and I had Maria, your Great Aunt Maria, who was always my soulmate, my great protector, and my dearest friend. She still is.

A few years later – I would have been nineteen or twenty by then – I had a job cutting cork in the forests near Maracha. I was on my own, and tired after a long day's work. I'd made myself a small fire, and after supper lay down beside it to sleep, the mules hobbled nearby. I fell asleep easily, and then I dreamed a strange dream, that Paco was lying there beside me, chewing the cud, licking his nose. He was so close I could smell his milky breath. I woke. Paco wasn't there. Of course he wasn't. It had been a dream. But as I got to my feet I noticed the grass nearby had been flattened. I felt it. It was warm. Then I saw hoof marks, the hoof marks of a massive bull. Paco had found me. We had found each other at last. The Black Phantom was no phantom. I called and I called for him, but he never came.

For years after that, whenever I worked the cork forests, I looked out for Paco, even though I knew it was quite impossible he could still be alive. But it didn't matter. Once was enough. I was a happy man.

* * * * *

My grandson's eyes had not left my face throughout the entire story, but after I'd finished he seemed to think there should be more.

"That was really the very worstest thing?" he asked. He sounded a little disappointed. "Didn't you ever break any windows?"

"I can't remember," I said. "I expect so."

The front door opened, and I heard his mother's voice. "I'm home," she called out. Antonito leapt off the bed.

"Secret, Antonito?" I said.

"Secret, Abuelo." He smiled at me, and was gone out of the room. By the time I reached the top of the stairs he was in his mother's arms, clinging to her.

"I'm sorry, Mum," he cried. "I'm really sorry." He looked up into her face.

"Mum, we won't ever be in a war, will we?"

"Of course not, Antonito."

"And you won't die, will you? You won't die?"

"Not for a while, I hope," she replied, and then she saw me standing there. "Abuelo, what brought all this on?"

I shrugged. "Who knows?" I said. "Who knows what goes on in the mind of a child?"